Published in Nashville, Tennessee, by Thomas Nelson. Thomas Nelson is a registered trademark of Thomas Nelson, Inc.

www.WhenSantaTurnedGreen.com

Thomas Nelson, Inc., titles may be purchased in bulk for educational, business, fund-raising, or sales promotional use. For information, please e-mail SpecialMarkets@ThomasNelson.com.

ISBN-13: 978-1-4003-1384-6

Library of Congress Control Number: 2008932992

Printed in the United States of America

08 09 10 11 12 WRZ 6 5 4 3 2 1

Dear Moms and Dads,

I wrote this story because I was searching for a non-scary way to tell my children about a serious issue. Not only did I want them to understand what global warming was about, I wanted them to feel that they could make a big impact right from their corner of the world—just by making lots of little changes.

And that's exactly what we've done, together. Simple changes such as walking home from school whenever possible; switching to refillable shampoo bottles in the shower; toting reusable drink containers; not idling the car; and yes, turning off the lights. Dad and I have also stepped it up by improving our home's energy efficiency and joining our town's clean power program.

The kids are excited about what we're doing and continue to come up with clever ideas of their own. I hope that my Green Santa will become your Green Santa and inspire the children in your life too. Tell us what you're doing by visiting www.WhenSantaTurnedGreen.com. We can't wait to hear what you're up to!

Have fun,

Vickie

P.S. This book is printed in the United States with soy-based inks on New Leaf Reincarnation paper, which is designated Ancient Forest Friendly and manufactured with electricity that is offset with Green-e® certified renewable energy certificates. It contains 100% recycled fiber which is 50% post-consumer waste, and processed chlorine-free. For more information, go to www.newleafpaper.com

This story was inspired by my brother
and his endless passion for a better planet & people.

This book is dedicated to my caring husband
and our two incredible children.
You are my healthy, thriving world.

When Santa Turned Green

By Victoria Perla

Illustrations By
Mirna Kantarevic

THOMAS NELSON
Since 1798

NASHVILLE   DALLAS   MEXICO CITY   RIO DE JANEIRO   BEIJING

It was just November,
but Santa's factory was already in
full gear.

The elves could feel each day getting **busier** and **busier.**

Mail was stacking up with notes from good girls and boys. The buzz of Christmas was starting to build.

That's when something really crazy happened.

Was it a jam in the die-cast car cranker?
A sprung sprocket in the mini-doll maker?

Nope.

It was a drop.
A simple, solitary drop of water.

Plop!

From the ceiling onto Santa's nose.

Santa pulled on his boots
and climbed up to the roof
of his snowy workshop to investigate.

A leak!

But that wasn't the only problem
Santa discovered that night.

The snow was melting.

On the
North Pole!

The land of permanent freeze
was getting soggier
by the minute.

Now this was a real problem.

How could **winter** be **winter**
without the cold?

And how could Christmas be Christmas
if it weren't dressed in white?

Santa had to get to the bottom of things.

And to do so, he climbed to the top.

The tippy top of the polar ice cap.

When Santa got there,
he couldn't believe his eyes.
The ice caps were shrinking in size.
Glaciers were slipping into the sea.

So he hopped into his sleigh
and set out to get some answers.

Santa learned that
this wasn't a **new** problem at all.
It had been building up
for a **very long time.**

Over the years, we Earthlings have been chopping down our forests. And pumping something called **carbon dioxide** into the sky. It comes from our **cars**...our **planes**... our **factories**...even our **chopped-down trees**.

And now there's so much of it
floating around Earth's atmosphere,
it's acting like a **big blanket** holding in the heat
of our planet—which makes temperatures go up, up, up.

Scientists call it **global warming.**

And when temperatures go up, our ice caps melt down.

"Global warming?!!"

Santa wondered if this was a task
too big for even him to tackle.
But Christmas... and the planet!
The future depended upon it!

So Santa went straight
to the future to solve it.

Did he jump into a time machine
and warp himself to the next millennium?
NO!

He went to the *real* future. *To you.*
And your sisters and brothers and friends.

That's right, he went to the children.
Because they have the power to change the world.

Santa knows the world's children better than anybody.
How **smart** they are. And how **good** they are.

(Remember, he's been checking that list
a looooOOOOooong time.)

But most of all,
he knows that when a child believes...
miracles happen.

And this time,
the world needed a **huge miracle.**

Can you imagine the commotion it caused to see Santa so early?!

Reindeer prints in November?

Sleighbells at Thanksgiving?!

But it wasn't toys that Santa was delivering.
It was a **call for help**. A message to the children
that they needed to **take action**.

And in return, the children gave Santa
the **greatest gift** he ever received.

Dylan walks to school—less fuel, more time to talk about life.

Ali convinced Grandpa to buy a hybrid.

They made lots of little changes, which made a World of difference.

Julia composts and recycles everything possible— slashed her family's trash in half!

Katie ditched disposable lunch containers for the reusable kind.

Lindsay started a school recycling program.

Paul plans to invent **new energy sources.**

Liam actually turns off lights when he leaves a room.

Ella picks toys that don't have to be shipped from far away.

Kiri plants a tree every month.

Even Santa made changes.
From energy efficient lighting
to wind and solar power for his factory.

Not to mention the green Santa suits
he asked Mrs. Claus to sew, for when
he sleigh rides 'round the world
making environmental checks on the planet.
He wears one every night
EXCEPT, OF COURSE,
Christmas Eve.

It took time, but after many years of persistence,
the "blanket" hanging around the planet thinned out

to something more like a **breezy curtain**.

The Earth's heat was finally able to slip off into space,

giving the glaciers, trees, oceans and environment

a much needed **breath of fresh air**.

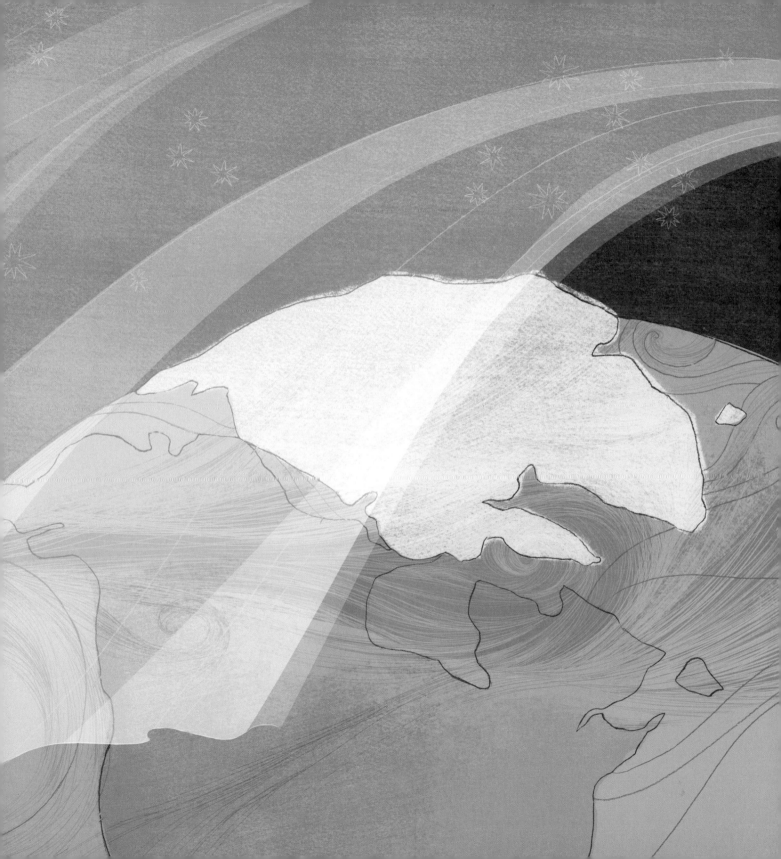

As for Santa,
his roof doesn't leak anymore.
Thanks to the help
of almost **two billion** children.

Victoria Perla is an award-winning advertising and freelance writer. She openly admits to being an idealist, which to this day fuels her childlike excitement for the magic of Christmas. Raised in New York City, she now lives with her family in New Jersey, where they welcome Santa all year 'round.

Mirna Kantarevic has been an artist since she was a young girl growing up in Bosnia. She studied illustration at the Ringling College of Art & Design in Sarasota, Florida, and looks forward to lending her visual magic to libraries of books.

This book would not be here today without the support of those who truly believed: Geri Brin (sounding board & friend), Lina Perl (one-woman think-tank), Chris Stubbs, Karen & Rick Leever, Colby Brin, Chad Peltola, David Segal, Peter Gardiner, Ken Frattini, Bonnie Sidler, Ed Chambliss, Todd Braverman, Eric Brown, John Bartlett, Beth Curley, Donyale Waithe, Claudia Sandoval, David Niggli, Ed Schmults, Laura Minchew, our families, and Paul . . . the one who believed from the very beginning.

My GReeN Ideas

by _____

* _____

* _____

* _____

* _____

* _____